THE MORGAN BAY MYSTERIES

The Mystery of Morgan Castle
The Mystery of the Marble Angel
The Mystery of the Midnight Visitor
The Mystery of the Missing Marlin

The Mystery

Gabby   Vinny

Illustrations by JOSEPH MANISCALCO

of

Morgan Castle

JOHN and NANCY RAMBEAU

Bill   Fritz   Miss Wellington

HARR WAGNER PUBLISHING COMPANY · SAN FRANCISCO

TABLE of CONTENTS

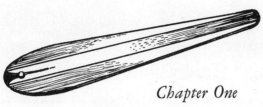

Chapter One

FRITZ RUNS AWAY

"I give up!" Gabby Summers said to his older brother. "I never will get a surfboard. I can't get a surfboard without money. I can't get any money if I don't have a job. And I can't get a job."

"Listen, Gabby," Bill said. "Never think *can't*. That's no way to get what you want. There are always jobs. But if you want one, you have to *think right*."

"Oh? And how do I think right?" Gabby said.

"Well, know what you want! Think of the job you want to have. Close your eyes," Bill said.

Gabby did as he was told.

"Now, think!" his brother went on. "Think of Gabby Summers doing that job."

"I'm thinking," Gabby said, with his eyes closed. "Yes, I can see it all now. I have a sitting-down job."

"You would!" Bill said.

He started looking through the Morgan Bay paper. Gabby opened his eyes. He saw Bill's hand moving down the paper. All at once, Bill's hand stopped.

"What did I say about right thinking? Listen to this," Bill said. "Wanted: Boy for dog-sitting. Call at 73 Board Walk."

"Oh, man! That was easy!" Gabby said. "But if it's *that* easy, why think about a job? Why can't I just think about *money*?"

"On your way, Gabby!" Bill said.

He started after his little brother. Gabby ran for the door.

"73 Board Walk—and think right!" Bill called after him.

Gabby started down the street. Board Walk was at the end of the street. Board Walk was not a street, but a walk along the beach. At last Gabby came to Board Walk and the sea wall. He looked over the sea wall at the surf.

He thought of the surfboard again. If only he had one now! He just had to have money for that surfboard.

He started along Board Walk. All along the beach were big, old houses. They had been there for years and years. Gabby was coming to the end of Board Walk. The walk ended at a high fence. He could see big, shaggy trees above the fence. Through the trees, he saw dark, empty windows and a high, pointed roof. Morgan Castle!

3

The Morgan house was older than all the others along Board Walk. Its high, pointed roof made it look like a castle. People in Morgan Bay had always called it Morgan Castle. Now some of its windows were broken. Others had boards over them. There was something frightening about the old house.

Gabby stopped. All at once he was afraid.

"Could 73 Board Walk be Morgan Castle?" he thought.

But, no. How could it be? Morgan Castle was empty. It had been empty for years. Gabby's family had been in Morgan Bay for a long time. But Morgan Castle had been empty all that time. All of the Morgan family were dead.

Gabby started walking again. At last he found 73 Board Walk. It was the last house—right before Morgan Castle.

The name on the door was *Wellington*. The Wellington house was almost as old as the Morgan house. To Gabby, it seemed almost as frightening. The sea wind was blowing through the shaggy trees at Morgan Castle. Gabby heard something banging in the wind.

Someone was moving around in the Wellington house. Gabby heard a dog on the other side of the door. The dog's nose was to the door. He sniffed at the door. Then he stopped sniffing and started to growl.

Gabby heard a tapping sound. Tap—tap—tap. It was coming closer and closer. Gabby started to feel more and more afraid. He had a feeling he was getting into something—something he was not going to like! The dog was still growling. Gabby wanted to run away. Just then, the door opened a little way.

"Stop it, Fritz! Stop it, now," a voice said.

An old lady stood there. In her hand was a long, dark cane. She looked at Gabby. Then she banged on the door with her cane.

"Be still, Fritz. It's all right," she said.

The big police dog stopped growling. The old lady took down the chain across the door.

7

"Now, then," she said to Gabby. "Did you come about the dog-sitting job? I am Miss Wellington—Miss Lucy Wellington. What is your name, boy?"

"Gabby, ma'am. Gabby Summers," said Gabby.

"Well," said the old lady. "Come in, can't you?"

She closed the door behind Gabby. Then she went on.

"I don't want people around this house. I'm all alone here. But I am going out of town for a day or two. I want someone to look after Fritz."

"Yes, ma'am," Gabby said. His eyes were on the big police dog.

"Now, don't be afraid of Fritz. He always growls at people he does not know," Miss Wellington said. "He will be all right when he knows you."

She took a long chain from the wall. She put it on the dog.

8

"It's time for Fritz's walk now. Come along with us so he will know you."

She opened the door and the dog jumped out.

"Don't move," Miss Wellington told Gabby. "And, above all, don't run."

Gabby could not have run if he had wanted to. He was feeling too frightened. The big police dog walked around him, sniffing and growling. Then the dog stopped growling.

Miss Wellington put the chain in Gabby's hand.

"Don't let go of the chain," she said. "If Fritz gets away, you will never get him back. And don't take him down on the beach. I don't want that sand in this house!"

Gabby said, "Yes, ma'am."

Then the trouble started!

The dog looked up. He saw a boy at the other end of the chain. He seemed to know Gabby could move fast. Then, with a bark, he was off.

He started to run, pulling Gabby after him. He ran across Board Walk. Then, with one jump, he was over the sea wall and on the sand!

Gabby did not let go of the chain. He jumped after Fritz. The big dog ran along the sand, pulling Gabby after him. It was all Gabby could do to keep from falling. He pulled and pulled on the chain. But Fritz ran on. Gabby could not stop him.

Then, all at once, the big dog stopped. Gabby went down in the sand, falling over Fritz. The dog stood still, sniffing. Then he started to growl.

Gabby heard Miss Wellington calling, "Fritz! Gabby! Come back here! Come back!"

Gabby looked around. He saw Miss Wellington watching them from the sea wall. Just then, the dog pulled at the chain. Before Gabby could stop him, he pulled away. Gabby's hand was empty. Dog and chain were gone!

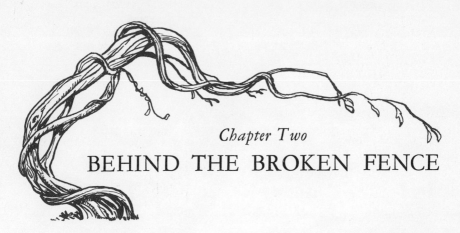

Chapter Two

BEHIND THE BROKEN FENCE

Gabby looked up. He was in front of Morgan Castle! Just then, he heard Fritz's high bark. It was coming from the other side of the fence. Fritz was in the garden of Morgan Castle!

Gabby looked up and down the beach. He saw an opening in the high fence. One of the boards had almost fallen down. Fritz had jumped through the opening!

There was nothing to do but go after the dog. Gabby could hear Fritz barking and growling in the garden. He climbed through the broken fence.

12

The garden had been left alone for years. It was nothing but a tangle of vines. Gabby stood still, looking at it. How could he get through the garden to Fritz? He started to make his way through the tangled vines. It was dark under the shaggy trees. He had to feel his way along. He climbed over one fallen branch after another.

At last Gabby saw the dog. Fritz had been running, pulling his long chain. But the chain had caught in the vines. It was so tangled that Fritz could not move.

Fritz stopped growling as Gabby came toward him. Just then, Gabby heard a sound from Morgan Castle. A door had opened and closed! Fritz growled again.

Gabby was frightened. He pulled and pulled at the tangled chain. At last the long vines came away from the chain. Fritz started to run toward the empty house. But this time he did not get away. Gabby caught the chain just in time.

13

"Oh, no," Gabby said. "Not this time. You are coming home!"

But Fritz was sniffing around through the vines. At last he found what he was looking for. It was only a paper bag.

"What do you have there?" Gabby said. "Give it to me."

He put his hand out for the bag. Fritz growled and Gabby pulled his hand back. Fritz was not going to give up that bag!

Gabby looked up at the dark, empty windows of Morgan Castle. He thought of the door, opening and closing. Someone was in the old castle!

Pulling Fritz after him, Gabby made his way back through the garden as fast as he could. He climbed back through the fence.

Miss Wellington was still waiting at the sea wall. Fritz jumped over the wall, the bag in his mouth. He put the bag down in front of Miss Wellington. He pushed the bag with his nose. Then he looked up at her.

"Someone is over there," Gabby said. "I think Fritz went after someone in that garden!"

Miss Wellington stood still, looking at the bag. Then her eyes moved to the empty windows of Morgan Castle. She seemed frightened.

She looked at Gabby.

"Did you see someone?" she said.

"No, ma'am," said Gabby. "But . . . ."

"Well, then," said the old lady. "Don't say things like that. Don't go around saying there is someone in that house. Do you hear me, Gabby?"

"Yes, ma'am," Gabby said.

"That house is empty—has been for years! I told you not to let go of Fritz's chain. You should have listened!" the old lady said.

She took Fritz and started into the house.

"Miss Wellington," Gabby called after her. "When are you going away?"

"I will not be going away," said Miss

16

Wellington. "And you will not have to come again."

She pulled Fritz into the house. The door banged behind them. Gabby was left there with his mouth open.

"Well—some dog-sitting job that was!" he thought. "What got into the old lady? She takes one look at the house—and bang! All at once, she is not going away. There *is* someone at the Morgan house. But why should she want me to keep still about it?"

Gabby looked at the bag. It was still where Fritz had left it. He put out his hand and picked it up. There was something in it! He opened the bag. Then his mouth opened again. In the bag were two twenty-dollar bills!

Chapter Three

NIGHT AT MORGAN CASTLE

Bill was waiting when Gabby came home. He wanted to hear about the dog-sitting job. But Gabby had other things to say.

"Listen!" he told Bill. "Something is going on in Morgan Castle."

He told Bill all about Miss Wellington. He told about Fritz going after someone in the garden. He handed him the twenty-dollar bills he had found.

"There is someone at Morgan Castle. I just know it," Gabby said. "But why did Miss Wellington say to keep still about it?"

Vinny, Gabby's older sister, had been listening.

"Miss Wellington!" she said, looking at Bill. "Lucy Wellington? Why, Morgan Castle is *her* house. The Morgans left it to her."

"Say, that's right!" Bill said. "She and

18

Ross Morgan were going to be married. Then he died. It seems to me I heard that Ross was always in trouble."

"That's what I heard, too," Vinny said. "His family let him have a car once. They say people jumped out of the way when they saw Ross's car coming. He went so fast, they were all frightened. But that car was the end of Ross!"

"Say, what *is* all this?" Gabby wanted to know. "Who was Ross Morgan? Was he one of the old Morgan family?"

"The *last* of the Morgan family!" said his sister. "One day Lucy ran away with him. She was years older than he was. But they were going to be married. Then the car ran off the road—right into the river. Someone saw the car in the river. They found Lucy on the road. She was hurt. She almost died. They thought she would never walk again. She still walks with a cane. But they never found Ross at all.

19

"The Morgans were good people," Vinny went on. "When they died, they left Morgan Castle to Lucy. They knew that she had almost married Ross."

"Miss Wellington closed up the house right after the Morgans died," said Bill. "No one has been in it for years."

"Someone is in that house now," Gabby said. "Someone left this money in the garden."

"Miss Wellington should know if someone is in Morgan Castle, Gabby," Bill said. "After all, it is her house. She told you it was empty. I think the wind was blowing that door open and closed. Fritz heard it, jumped into the garden, and found the bag of money."

"Well," said Vinny. "I don't know how the money got into the garden. But we can't keep it. Gabby will have to take it back."

"Why?" Gabby wanted to know. "I bet that's not even Miss Wellington's money. It's just some old money her dog found. I want that money for a surfboard."

"You can't keep it," Bill said. "After all it did come from Miss Wellington's house."

"Oh, all right," Gabby said. "But I can't take it back now. Look—it's getting dark."

Gabby pointed to the window. He thought of Miss Wellington looking at the dark, empty windows of Morgan Castle. If no one was in the castle, why had she seemed so frightened? And all at once, she was not going away. Why?

That night Gabby could not stop thinking. He was not thinking about money now. He was thinking about the mystery at Morgan Castle. He looked over at his brother. Bill's eyes were closed. Gabby got up and put on his things. Without making a sound, he moved to the window. He climbed through it into the garden. Then Gabby started down the dark street.

He was almost to the end of the street when he heard someone behind him.

Gabby looked around. He saw his older brother coming down the street.

"What do you think you are doing? Where are you going alone at this time of night?" Bill said.

"Listen," Gabby said. "I *know* someone is in Morgan Castle. I'm going to find out who it is."

"Gabby!" Bill said. "You can't nose around that house alone."

"Well—come with me, why don't you? Then I will not be alone," said Gabby. "Come on. We can just go and look around."

He started walking down the street again. His brother walked after him.

"So there was someone in the garden! So what?" Bill said. "I bet he is not there now. We could get into trouble or something, nosing around at night. Come on, Gabby, we had better go home."

"You can go home if you want to," Gabby said. "But I'm going to Morgan Castle."

Bill watched Gabby walk down the street. At last he went after him. He knew he could not let his brother go to the castle alone.

All of the windows in Morgan Bay were dark. There was not a light to be seen. The two boys came to the sea wall. They climbed over it to the beach. There they walked along the sand, not making a sound. Even so, Gabby heard Fritz bark when they went by Miss Wellington's.

At last they came to the fence in front of Morgan Castle. Above them was the castle's high, pointed roof.

"Look there," Gabby said to Bill. "Do you see that board? When I was here, that board was down. Now someone has put it back again. You see? Someone *is* in that house."

"All right, all right," Bill said. "But how do we get into the garden? We can't get through the fence here."

"There are gates in back," Gabby said. "We can go around the other side of Morgan Castle to the back."

They walked around the castle. At last they were on the street behind the castle. The big gates were closed. There seemed no way to open them.

"The gates are closed," Bill said. "And we can't climb over that high fence. Why don't we go home now?"

Gabby pulled him over to a tree by the fence.

"Climb up here," he said. "It will be easy. We can see over the fence from that branch."

Bill made his way up the tree. Gabby came after him. The two boys climbed along the branch. They looked down into the dark, tangled garden.

"Bill!" Gabby said. "Look—over there! Do you see what I see?"

Chapter Four

A LIGHT IN THE BASEMENT

"A truck!" Gabby said. "What is a truck doing at Morgan Castle?"

"Look," Bill said. "There are some old branches and things on that truck. That's a gardener's truck, Gabby. That's your mystery man—the gardener. Now, what do you say we go home?"

"Gardener!" Gabby said. "If he is a gardener, he is not doing a thing to *this* garden. You should see this garden in the light of day! Listen, Bill—something is going on in that house. Someone is in there. I know someone is in there."

"All right. Have it your way," Bill said.

"It's not the gardener. But this is not *your* house. If someone is in there, it's nothing to you—and nothing to me. I am going home."

With that, Bill climbed back along the branch and started down the tree.

All at once he heard his brother say, "Bill! Come back!"

Bill looked up. Gabby was sitting dead still. He was watching something in the garden. Bill climbed up again. He looked through the branches and over the fence.

Someone was walking toward the truck— a man. There was a box in his hands. He put the box in the back of the truck under the branches. Another man came out of the old house with another box. As the boys watched, the two men put box after box in the truck. They put more branches over the boxes. Then the men went back to the house. The boys heard a door close.

"You see?" Gabby said. "I knew something was going on! I think they went into the basement. Maybe we can see them through the basement windows."

"Take it easy," said Bill. "Listen! They are coming back again."

Again came the sound of the door opening and closing. The two men started across the garden. One climbed into the truck. The other opened the big gates. He was right by the branch the boys were on.

The truck started. The boys watched as it pulled through the gate and stopped. After closing the gate, the other man climbed into the truck. Away it went, up the street.

Gabby climbed down into the dark garden.

"Watch out!" Bill said, behind him. "Maybe there are more than two. Someone could still be in that basement. If we get caught, we *will* be in trouble."

Without a sound, the boys moved through the tangled vines. They climbed over the broken branches. Closer and closer they came to the basement windows. Then Bill put out a hand to stop Gabby. Someone had put boards across one of the windows. But through the opening between the boards they saw a light.

Someone was still in the basement! The boys heard someone moving around.

Gabby moved toward the light. He started to look between the boards. But if there was something to see—Gabby never saw it. One of the old boards came down with a bang.

The boys jumped back from the window.

They heard a man walking across the basement. They heard him open the door. He was coming out—coming out to the garden to look for them!

Bill had taken Gabby's hand. Now he pulled his brother away from the house. He pulled Gabby with him into the trees. They just had time to move behind the tangled vines. There they waited, not moving—not making a sound.

They saw the man walking along the side of the house. At the basement window he stopped. He stood looking about the garden— listening.

Just then, Fritz started to bark.

"That dog!" the boys heard the man say. "If he comes over here again, I'm. . . ."

What he said after that, the boys could not hear. The man picked up the board. He put it up to the window again. After another look around the dark garden, he went back as he had come.

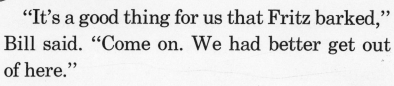

"It's a good thing for us that Fritz barked," Bill said. "Come on. We had better get out of here."

There was no way of getting over the back fence from the garden. The boys started through the trees toward the sea. They found where the fence had been broken. They pulled at the board. At last they made an opening in the fence. Then they climbed down to the beach.

Gabby looked back at the fence.

"Do you think we should have pulled the board back?" he said. "Do you think we should make it look the way it looked before?"

"No," said Bill. "Now it will look even more as if Fritz had been in the garden."

"You see?" Gabby said as they walked along. "There is something going on."

"I think there is a mystery at Morgan Castle," Bill said. "But I don't know what to do about it."

The boys looked back at the castle as they walked along the beach. All at once Gabby stopped walking.

"Look!" Gabby said. "There by the sea wall! That's Lucy Wellington. Do you think she saw us?"

The old lady stood there, not moving. She seemed to be watching, listening for something. Then her voice came to them on the sea wind.

"Fritz! Fritz, where are you? Come back, Fritz," she was calling.

Had Fritz run away again? Had he gone into the garden at Morgan Castle? All at once Gabby was afraid—afraid that Fritz would never come out of that dark garden.

The boys climbed the sea wall and started for home. Gabby heard Miss Wellington calling again, as they went up the street.

"Come home, Fritz! Come home."

Then—nothing. Nothing but the sound of the sea wind and the surf behind them.

Chapter Five

GABBY FINDS FRITZ

The boys told Vinny about the truck they had seen the night before. They told her about the three men. She wanted to call the police.

"But we can't," Bill said. "Not now. After all, we can't just say, 'We *think.*' We have to *know.*"

"That's right," Gabby said to his sister. "The police will not listen. And that will be the end of that."

"I think we should take one more look around. Come on, Gabby," Bill said. "I think we had better go down to Morgan Castle again."

"If you go, I'm going, too," said Vinny.

"Oh, no," Bill said. "This is no job for you."

Vinny watched the boys walk down the street.

36

"Maybe nosing around that house is no job for me. But there should be something I can do," she thought. "I know! I bet I can find out more about Lucy Wellington. Maybe —just maybe—the mystery has something to do with her!"

Bill had taken the back of Morgan Castle to watch. Gabby had taken the front. He walked along the beach. This time, as he went by Miss Wellington's, he did not hear Fritz. Without Fritz's bark, Miss Lucy's house seemed as empty as the castle.

Gabby looked up at the high fence in front of Morgan Castle. Was the board back again? He knew it would be, almost without looking —and it was.

Gabby started to think Bill had taken the better job. There was little to be seen from the beach. He could see the pointed castle roof. He saw a window or two, through the shaggy trees. But there was no way of seeing the basement windows—or the garden.

Gabby waited on the beach. He listened to the sea wind and watched the surf. He did not know how long he had been watching when he saw something! It was something dark, moving in and out on the surf. Now it was almost up on the sand. And now the surf had pulled it out again.

Gabby walked across the sand. Something told him what he was going to find. The closer it came, the more afraid he was. At last, he stood close to the surf. He watched the dark thing moving toward him.

It was Fritz! He was dead!

The man in the basement had caught Fritz. And now Fritz was dead. What if Bill were caught nosing around? What would the man do to Bill? Would Bill get hurt?

His sister had been right. They should not have come here alone. They should have called the police.

Gabby thought of Miss Wellington. He thought of her calling for Fritz the night before. Did she know why Fritz had not come home? No. The old lady had trouble walking. She could not have walked across the sand.

Gabby would have to let her know about Fritz. He ran for the sea wall.

Miss Wellington did not come to the door. Gabby listened for the tap of the long cane. But he heard nothing. Not a sound came from the house.

Where could the old lady be? Could she have left town after all? Or could she have gone out looking for Fritz? Gabby looked

39

down Board Walk. There was no Miss Wellington to be seen. Board Walk was empty. Was the house empty, too?

"Miss Wellington could still be in the house. Maybe she can't make it to the door," Gabby thought. "Maybe she has fallen down. She could be hurt. Maybe I should go in and see if I can help her."

He put his hand on the door. It opened, but only a little way.

"The chain is still on the door! She should be in the house," thought Gabby.

He pushed his hand through the opening. At last he found a way to take down the chain. He went in. Waiting by the door, he called her name, "Miss Wellington! Miss Wellington!"

But even as he called, he knew she was not there. There was an empty sound—an empty feeling about the house. Gabby knew he was alone. All at once he was afraid—afraid for Miss Wellington.

Chapter Six
TWO IN TROUBLE

"Miss W-Wellington?" Gabby called again in a frightened voice. "Are you here? Are you all right?"

But Gabby heard not a sound in the old house.

He started making his way through the rooms. As he went from one room to another, he was afraid—afraid of what he would find behind the doors. But he found nothing.

There were still the rooms above. Gabby did not think Miss Wellington went up there. She would have trouble getting up and down. Still, he had to look.

As he had thought, the rooms above had been closed for a long time—all but one. It was one of the back rooms. The door to this one stood open. Gabby could see that some-one had been in the room. Gabby walked to the window. He saw at once why Miss Wel-lington had come up to this room. From the window, she could look over the fence and through the shaggy trees. She could see into the castle garden.

Gabby looked down into Miss Welling-ton's little back garden. There was a back gate that opened to the street behind. Then, behind some tangled vines, Gabby saw an-other gate! This gate was in the high fence between the Wellington house and Morgan Castle. It opened into the castle garden. The old gate looked as if it had been closed for years. But now—it stood open!

Had Miss Wellington gone to Morgan Castle? If so, she had not come back! And where was Bill?

"I have to find Bill. I have to find Bill," Gabby said over and over. "I have to find Bill. He will know what to do."

Gabby ran as fast as he could. He ran down to Lucy Wellington's back door. He ran through her garden to the back gate. Pulling it open, he looked up and down the street. Bill should have been there. He was not.

Gabby stood looking at the empty street. He was feeling more and more afraid. Where could Bill be? Was he in trouble? Had he been caught?

Gabby went back into Miss Wellington's garden. He saw the other gate still open. Something seemed to pull him toward the open gate—toward the castle garden on the other side.

Gabby looked through the opening. The garden looked empty. But there was no way of knowing who was in the basement, watching. He got down and started through the garden. He moved without a sound, keeping behind the tangled vines. Closer and closer he moved toward the old house. Then he saw it!

There, almost under his nose, was Miss
Wellington's cane.

"She *did* come over here," Gabby thought.
"And the men caught her. I know it!"

Now Gabby knew he had to call the police.
He had to get out of that garden. And fast!
He started for the side gate again. But just
then he heard something. A door banged. A
man had come out of the basement. He was
walking toward the big gates.

Gabby did not move. If a branch moved,
the man would look his way. Then Gabby
heard the truck. A truck was coming down
the street. He heard it stop on the other side
of the big gates. He watched the man from
the basement open the gates. Now the truck
pulled into the garden. The gates were closed
again.

Gabby could see into the back end of the truck. He saw that the old branches were still on the truck. But the boxes did not seem to be under the branches.

The man who had come from the basement was moving toward the two men in the truck. Now he was between Gabby and the truck. Gabby could hear what he was saying.

"What took you so long? Listen, Morgan. It's time we got out of here."

Morgan! Gabby's eyes opened when he heard that name. What could this man have to do with the Morgan family?

"Get out of here? Why?" said Morgan, climbing from the truck. "Who is going to find us here?"

"Someone has found us," said the other. "It's the old lady. I caught her over here."

"Lucy? She will not give us any trouble. I told you that," said Morgan.

Gabby's mouth opened.

What did Lucy Wellington have to do with

this man? To Gabby, listening, it was more and more of a mystery.

"Look," Morgan went on. "This job is almost over. This is no time to get frightened."

"No?" said the other man. "Then what about the boy?"

Gabby put his hand over his mouth. He was afraid to make a sound.

"There was a boy nosing around the back gates. There was nothing to do but put him in the basement. What are we going to do with them—the old lady and the boy?"

Morgan stood thinking. "Nothing—here. Put them in the back of the truck. We will take them with us. We will have to find a better house than this after all."

"Right! Come on. I will get the other boxes. You see to the boy and the old lady. We have to get out of here fast!"

Chapter Seven

THREE IN A BASEMENT

Vinny walked to the window again. The boys had been gone for a long time. She looked down the street once more. It was still empty.

She picked up the bag Gabby had found. She looked at one of the twenty-dollar bills.

"What could this have to do with the mystery at Morgan Castle?" she thought.

She looked at one of the twenty-dollar bills again.

"J-A-C-K-S-O- - -N," she said. "Now. . . ."

All at once Vinny's eyes opened. She put down the money. She knew now what she had to do.

At Morgan Castle Gabby was watching the three men walk toward the basement. Now he could not hear what they were saying. But he knew that he had to move fast.

"If I can only get to the truck," he thought. "I have to stop the men before they take Bill and Miss Wellington away."

He knew that if he were caught it would be the end for all of them. But the men had gone into the basement. And the truck was between Gabby and the basement window.

"The tires," he thought. "I have to get to one of the back tires."

Little by little he made his way toward the truck. He was listening for the basement door. Now his

hand was on the back tire. He found what he was looking for. Ss-ss-ss-sssss. The tire was going down.

"The men can't go with the tire like this," Gabby thought. "This tire will keep the men from getting out fast. Now I will have time— time to call the police."

He moved away, keeping behind the truck. He started to make his way back to the side gate through the tangled vines.

Then, all at once, Gabby heard the sound of a door opening and closing. Someone was coming toward him. This time there would not be Fritz's barking to help him. Gabby started to run.

"I see you!" a voice called out. "Stop! Stop right where you are, if you don't want to get hurt."

Gabby looked back at the man coming toward him. It was the man called Morgan! Gabby could not run any more. He was too frightened.

"All right," Morgan said. "What are you doing nosing around here? You had better come with me."

The man took Gabby into the basement of Morgan Castle. The other two men were watching them as they came in. Gabby saw Miss Wellington and Bill on the other side of the room. They seemed to be all right.

"What? Another one?" a man was saying.

"Just move the boxes out of here," Morgan told him. "If any more people come around here, there will not be room in the truck. Go on. I will watch the three here."

"Now what are you going to do with the three of us, Ross Morgan?" Miss Wellington called out.

"Ross?" Gabby's mouth was open. He looked at his brother.

"Ha! Ha!" Morgan said. "I bet I fooled you. I bet you thought I was dead. All the people in this town think I am. It was so easy to fool this town. Ha! Ha! Ha!"

"You did not fool me, Ross Morgan," Miss Wellington said. "I knew you were not dead. For more than twenty years I have been keeping still."

Miss Wellington looked at Gabby.

"It was the day we were to be married," she told him. "Ross's car went off the old River Road."

Then she looked again at Morgan.

"*I saw you,*" she said. "I could not move, but I was watching you. I saw you push the car into the river. And then I saw you walk down the road."

"You *pushed* the car?" Bill said.

"Yes," Morgan said. "I wanted to get out of this town. I never liked it here. What could I do here? Nothing. I did not want to get married. And it was so easy. The car was almost off the road. It only took two or three pushes. Then the car was all the way off the road and into the river. And then I left town. Yes, I had to get out."

The men had taken all of the boxes out to the truck. Then one of the men came back.

"The back tire is down, Morgan. We will have to put on another one."

"Well, get going," Morgan told him. "We are having nothing but trouble here."

Morgan looked at Lucy Wellington.

"So," he said to her. "You knew I was not dead. Why did you keep still about it?"

"What was I to say to your family?" Lucy said. "Could I say that you were not dead? Could I say that you pushed the car into the river so they would think you were? Could I say that you had run away? No. Your family was too good for that. I could not hurt them. And when they died. . . ."

Ross Morgan moved over to the door. He looked out to see how the men were doing. Then he looked at Lucy.

"Why do you think people in this town look up to the name of Morgan?" Lucy went on. "You know as well as I, Ross. There was

a time when there was no money in Morgan Bay. There were no jobs. All of the people went to your family for help. And I never knew them to say no to any man. Yes, it was the Morgan family that pulled this town through. I did not want you to hurt the Morgan name."

"This is nothing to me," Ross Morgan said.

"I know," Lucy said. "But I have waited for more than twenty years. I always thought you would come back and start over. Then last night I saw something. I watched one of your men take Fritz out of the garden. I could see that Fritz was dead. I knew then that you were up to something. And I knew that you would never start over."

Lucy stopped. Then she went on.

"You thought I would always keep still, Ross. You thought I was a fool. But now you are the one who is fooled. Do you think I came over here without calling the police?"

Ross started toward Miss Wellington.

"Don't move, Morgan!" a voice from the
garden called out. "And put up your hands!"

Then Gabby saw a man at the door.

"The police!" Gabby said. "Oh, man—it's
a good thing you came."

Gabby looked at Miss Wellington. But she
was looking at the policeman.

"H-How did you get here?" she said.

Chapter Eight

AN EMPTY CASTLE

"Well, Morgan," the policeman said. "We have been looking for you a long time. We never thought that the man we wanted was a 'dead' man."

Morgan did not say a thing. He stood still, looking at Miss Wellington.

"It's this town," he said then. "I never had any trouble before. I never should have come back here. All I found in this town was trouble."

The policeman looked at the other three in the basement.

"It's a good thing that you are all right. Morgan can't give you any more trouble—not where he is going."

The policeman took Morgan away. Gabby and Bill helped Miss Wellington out of the basement.

"But, how did the police get here?" she said.

"You said you called the police," Gabby said.

Miss Wellington put her hand over her eyes. Then she took her hand away.

"I only told Ross I did. I wanted to frighten him," she said. "I wanted a little time to think. I thought I would think of something to do."

They started to walk through the garden. The police were moving toward the back gates with Morgan and his two men. Another policeman was picking up little papers that were blowing across the garden and through the trees. One of the boxes had fallen off the truck. The little papers were blowing out of the box.

Gabby put out his hand. He picked up one of the blowing papers.

"Bill—look here!" he said. "Money! There are twenty-dollar bills all over the garden—

even in the trees. You see? That's what comes of thinking about money. Man, it's a good thing you told me about right thinking."

The policeman who was picking up the money heard Gabby.

"Oh, oh!" he said. "I am afraid you can't keep that. You had better give it to me. If you got caught with *that* money, you would be in trouble. It's no good."

"No good?" Gabby said. "But—but...."

"No good at all!" the policeman told him. "That's what Morgan and his men were making in the basement. And that's why they are in trouble."

The boys watched the policeman walk away. Bill looked at Gabby.

"Do something for me, will you?" he said. "Stop thinking. You frighten me."

"Gabby! Bill! Miss Wellington!" a voice called out.

It was Vinny. She was coming across the garden.

"You are all right!" she said. "I did not know if the police were going to get here in time."

"You?" Gabby said to his sister. "Did you call the police?"

Vinny looked at Miss Wellington. "I thought the mystery had something to do with you," she told the old lady. "So I went into town to look through some of the old Morgan Bay papers. I looked all day. But I did not find a thing that helped. All the time what I should have been looking for was at home."

To Bill and Gabby, it was still a mystery.

"I looked at one of the twenty-dollar bills you found in the garden, Gabby," Vinny

65

went on. "All at once I saw something. What I saw was 'Jackso.' It should have said 'Jackson.' So I knew it was not good. Then I called the police. The police wanted to hear what I had to say."

"The police should have been called long before now," Miss Wellington said. "They should have been called when the Morgans died—even before the Morgans died. I should not have been still all this time."

Miss Wellington looked back at the empty castle. Gabby looked, too. Morgan Castle did not seem frightening any more. It was just a home without any family. Under the high, pointed roof, its dark, empty windows seemed like eyes—watching for someone who would never come. Where once there had been voices, only the sea wind called through the tangled garden.

Gabby found Miss Wellington's cane. Then the three of them helped Miss Wellington home. At last they started along Board Walk.

66

Bill looked over the sea wall at the surf.

"Miss Wellington has had her troubles, all right," he said. "If only there were something we could do for her! She seems so alone in that big house."

"Think how it hurt her when Ross ran away," said Gabby. "But she was too good to hurt the Morgans."

"It's a good thing she never married Ross. She is better off without him," Vinny said. "How could a man like that come from a family like the Morgans?"

"It's not what your family is—it's what *you* are!" Gabby told her.

"Right," said Bill. "That's something to think about."

"I don't think I want to think," Gabby said. "I'm through thinking. I thought 'money, money, money' for days. And all I got were some no-good twenty-dollar bills. I still don't have a surfboard. I don't even have a job any more."

Vinny and Bill looked at one another. Gabby had his troubles, too. There seemed no way to help him.

Then all at once Gabby said, "I have it! It just came to me! I know how I can get that job back again. Then I can get a surfboard. And Miss Wellington will not be alone any more. It's easy. All I have to do is get Miss Wellington another *dog!*"

EXERCISES

Chapter One

FRITZ RUNS AWAY

Which Is Right?

Read each sentence below. Does the chapter you have read say it is true? On your paper, write only those sentences that are true.

1. Bill wanted a surfboard because he had to have the money.
2. Gabby is older than his brother Bill.
3. The big old houses along the beach had been there for years and years.
4. Gabby's family had been in Morgan Castle a long time.
5. The Wellington house was almost as old as Morgan Castle.
6. Gabby started sniffing at the door.
7. Miss Wellington was going away for a day or two.
8. Miss Wellington said she wanted sand in the house.
9. Fritz seemed to know that Gabby could run faster than Miss Wellington.

The Mystery of the Missing Word

Choose the right word or words for each sentence.

1. The Morgan Bay paper said, "Wanted: Boy for _____."
   (moving) (Board Walk) (dog-sitting)

2. Board Walk was a _____.
   (sea wall)   (street)   (walk)   (board)

3. The windows of Morgan Castle were _____.
   (shaggy)   (dark)   (pointed)

4. Its high pointed roof made it look like a _____.
   (tree)   (castle)   (brother)   (73)

5. In Miss Wellington's hand was a long, dark ____.
   (police dog)   (door)   (chain)   (cane)

6. Fritz always _____ at people he does not know.
   (jumps)   (growls)   (runs)   (taps)

7. Miss Wellington opened the door and _____
   jumped out.
   (Gabby)   (Bill)   (Fritz)

8. _____ started to run, pulling Gabby after him.
   (The wind)   (Miss Wellington)   (Fritz)

9. _____ stood still, sniffing.
   (Miss Wellington)   (Bill)   (Fritz)   (Gabby)

To Think about and Talk about

1. If you wanted a surfboard, how would you get the money?

2. What things frightened Gabby about the house at 73 Board Walk?

3. Why do you think Fritz began to growl on the beach, then pulled away from Gabby?

4. Bill said that the right kind of thinking could help Gabby get a job. Do you think he was right?

Chapter Two

BEHIND THE BROKEN FENCE

Who Did What?

Choose the right word or words for each sentence.

1. _____ was barking and growling in the garden.
(Bill) (Gabby) (Miss Wellington) (Fritz)

2. _____ took the paper bag to Miss Wellington.
(Gabby) (Fritz)

3. _____ told Gabby not to let go of Fritz's chain.
(Someone) (Fritz) (Miss Wellington)

4. _____ went into the garden after Fritz.
(Miss Wellington) (Someone) (Gabby)

Why?

Choose the right ending for each sentence below. Then write the sentence on your paper. Do not look at the chapter.

1. Gabby went into the garden after Fritz because
(a) Miss Wellington was watching.
(b) he wanted to find a paper bag.
(c) he had to get the dog back.
(d) there was too much sand on the beach.

2. Fritz ran away because
(a) he was afraid of Gabby.
(b) his chain was broken.
(c) he knew someone was in the garden.
(d) he wanted to jump in the vines.

74

3. Gabby knew Morgan Castle was not empty because
   (a) the fence was broken.
   (b) Fritz's chain was caught in the door.
   (c) the house was at the end of Board Walk.
   (d) he heard a door open and close.
4. Miss Wellington told Gabby not to come back because
   (a) she wanted an older boy.
   (b) he talked too fast.
   (c) she was not going away after all.

WHAT WOULD YOU HAVE DONE?

1. When Fritz pulled away and ran into the garden of Morgan Castle?
2. If you had heard a door open and close in a house you had thought was empty?
3. When Miss Wellington told you not to come back?
4. If you found a paper bag with two twenty-dollar bills in it?

Chapter Three

NIGHT AT MORGAN CASTLE

<small>SAME OR DIFFERENT?</small>

Number your paper from 1 to 18. If each of the two words on the same line mean the same, or almost the same, put an S after the number. If they mean different things, put a D.

1. dark—light
2. dollar—money
3. right—left
4. listened—heard
5. still—moving
6. cane—car
7. brother—sister
8. open—close
9. think—start

10. beach—sand
11. gate—tangle
12. branch—tree
13. watch—look
14. always—never
15. road—street
16. window—gate
17. fence—wall
18. sea—see

<small>WHO IS WHO?</small>

The people in the story are Gabby, Bill, Vinny, Lucy Wellington and Ross Morgan. Number your paper from 1 to 9, and after each number write the name of the person that answers the question.

1. Who is Gabby's sister?
2. Who does Morgan Castle belong to?
3. Who almost married Ross Morgan?
4. Who was found on the road after the car went into the river?
5. Who is Gabby's older brother?

76

6. Who came after Gabby when he climbed out of the window and started to the castle?
7. Who was the last of the Morgan family?
8. Who told Gabby he would have to take the money back to Miss Wellington?
9. Who was afraid of getting into trouble by going to the empty castle at night?

BIG WORDS FROM LITTLE WORDS

Each word in List A *fits with a word in* List B *to make a new word. Write these new words on your paper.*

A	B
with	round
some	to
in	one
surf	thing
some	board
a	out

TO THINK ABOUT AND TALK ABOUT

1. What things make you think someone is in the old Morgan house?
2. Why do you think Miss Wellington told Gabby to keep still about hearing someone in the garden?

Chapter Four

A LIGHT IN THE BASEMENT

WHICH CAME FIRST?

Read each pair of sentences below. Choose the sentence in each pair that happened first. Write it on your paper after each number.

1. A man came out of the house with another box.
   Gabby saw the gardener's truck.
2. The boys saw a light in the basement.
   A man closed the gate and walked to the truck.
3. Gabby started to look between the boards.
   The board came down with a bang.
4. The boys heard a man in the basement.
   The boys heard Fritz barking.
5. The boys climbed down to the beach.
   Bill looked through the branches at the truck.
6. The boys heard Miss Wellington calling Fritz.
   The boys found where the fence was broken.
7. Miss Wellington stood by the sea wall.
   Bill and Gabby started for home.

FIND THE RIGHT WORD

Choose the right word or words for each sentence. Then write the sentence on your paper.

1. On the back of the gardener's truck were some old _____.
   (ladies)   (police dogs)   (branches)   (windows)

2. The men put the boxes in the back of the _____.
   (gate)   (boys)   (fence)   (truck)

3. The boys climbed down into the dark _____.
   (basement)   (roof)   (boards)   (garden)

4. Bill pulled Gabby with him into the _____.
   (dog)   (truck)   (sea wall)   (surf)   (trees)

5. The vines in the garden were _____.
   (jumping)   (tangled)   (barking)   (alone)

6. The boys knew there was a _____ at Morgan Castle.
   (lady)   (beach)   (bang)   (mystery)

7. As they walked along the beach the boys looked back at the _____.
   (light)   (sea)   (mystery)   (castle)   (branches)

8. Miss Wellington was standing by the _____.
   (sea wall)   (surf)   (basement)   (truck)

9. She was calling _____.
   (Ross Morgan)   (Vinny)   (Gabby)   (Fritz)

10. The boys climbed the sea wall and started
    _____.
    (barking)   (calling)   (pulling)   (home)

To Think about and Talk about

1. What things have happened so far in the story that seem to be a mystery?
2. Why was it a good thing that Fritz barked when he did?
3. What might have happened if the man had caught Bill and Gabby?

Chapter Five

GABBY FINDS FRITZ

Which Is Right?

Read each sentence below. Does the chapter you have read say it is true? On your paper, write only those sentences that are true.

1. The boys told Vinny about the truck.
2. Vinny thought the mystery had something to do with Fritz.
3. Gabby waited on the roof.
4. Gabby saw Miss Wellington moving in and out on the surf.
5. Fritz was dead.
6. Miss Wellington could not have walked across the sand.
7. Gabby had to tell Miss Wellington about her surfboard.
8. Gabby listened for the tap of the long chain.
9. Gabby had a feeling there was someone in Miss Wellington's house.

Who Did It?

On your paper, write the name of the person in the story who did it.

1. _____ wanted to call the police.
2. _____ watched the back of the castle.
3. _____ found the board had been put back in the fence again.

4. _____ waited on the beach.
5. _____ saw the thing in the surf.
6. _____ had trouble walking.
7. _____ did not come to the door.
8. _____ took the chain away from Miss Wellington's door.
9. _____ was afraid for Miss Wellington.
10. _____ listened for the tap of the long cane.

To Think about and Talk about

1. Do you think the boys should have told the police about what they saw in the garden?
2. Why did they think it would be better to wait and tell the police later?
3. What happened that made Gabby think they should have called the police?
4. If you had been Gabby, what would you have done when you found Fritz?
5. Would you have gone into Miss Wellington's house to look for her? Why? Why not?

Chapter Six

TWO IN TROUBLE

Remember Why

Choose the right ending for each sentence below. Then write the sentence on your paper. Do not look at the chapter.

1. At first Gabby did not think Miss Wellington would have gone to the rooms above because
   (a) there was too much wind up there.
   (b) the rooms had been closed a long time.
   (c) she had trouble getting up and down.

2. Miss Wellington had climbed to the room above because
   (a) she was looking for her cane.
   (b) she wanted to watch the surf.
   (c) she wanted to look over the fence into the castle garden.

3. Gabby ran to find Bill because
   (a) he thought Bill would know what to do.
   (b) he thought Bill was taking it easy.
   (c) Bill was with Miss Wellington.
   (d) Bill had Miss Wellington's surfboard.

4. Gabby knew Miss Wellington had gone to Morgan Castle because
   (a) he saw her sitting in the truck.
   (b) Bill told him.
   (c) he heard her calling.
   (d) he found her cane in the castle garden.

82

5. Gabby could not get out of the garden to call the police because
   (a) he was caught in the vines.
   (b) the gate was open.
   (c) the men would have seen him if he moved.
6. Gabby was frightened because
   (a) the man in the truck was named Morgan.
   (b) he saw so many boxes in the truck.
   (c) the men in the basement had Bill and Miss Wellington.

How Are They the Same?

These things are alike in some way. Tell how each pair of things is alike.

1. A board and a tree
2. A door and a gate
3. A fence and a wall
4. A tap and a push
5. A vine and a branch
6. A box and a room

To Think about and Talk about

If you were Gabby, how do you think you would stop the men from taking Bill and Miss Wellington away in the truck?

Chapter Seven

THREE IN A BASEMENT

WHAT HAPPENED FIRST?

Each of these things happened in the chapter you have just read, but they are mixed up here. On your paper, write them as they happened.

1. The men took Gabby into the basement.
2. Vinny looked at the twenty-dollar bills.
3. The police came.
4. Gabby let the air out of the truck tire.
5. The men took all the boxes out to the truck.

WHICH ONE SAID IT?

Which one of the people in the story said each of these sentences? You may look at the chapter.

1. "What are you doing nosing around here?"
2. "Now what are you going to do with the three of us, Ross Morgan?"
3. "Ha! Ha! I bet I fooled you."
4. "I could not move, but I was watching you."
5. "Don't move, Morgan!"

TELL WHO DID IT

Can you remember who did these things? Number your paper from 1 to 7 and put down the right name after each number. Do not look at the chapter.

1. Who caught Gabby in the garden of the castle?

2. Who knew Ross Morgan was not dead all those years?
3. Who pushed Ross's car into the river?
4. Who wanted to get out of Morgan Bay?
5. Who did not want to hurt Ross's family?
6. Who thought Lucy Wellington was a fool?
7. Who thought he would have time to call the police?

To Think about and Talk about

1. Vinny thought the twenty-dollar bills had something to do with the mystery at Morgan Castle. Do you? In what way?
2. Why do you think Ross Morgan turned out the way he did?
3. Why did Lucy Wellington think it was better to let people think Ross Morgan was dead?
4. Can you think why it was *not* right of her to do so?
5. Do you think Ross Morgan would have hurt Miss Wellington if the police had not come? Why, or why not?

Chapter Eight

AN EMPTY CASTLE

Find the Mystery Word

Choose the right word or words for each sentence.

1. The policemen took _____ away.
   (Morgan Castle) (Vinny) (Ross Morgan)

2. _____ was blowing around in the garden.
   (A policeman) (A box) (Jackson) (Money)

3. Morgan and his men were making money in the _____.
   (town) (river) (garden) (basement)

4. Gabby wanted to _____ the money.
   (keep) (watch) (blow) (give away)

5. The empty castle was not _____ any more.
   (empty) (jumping) (frightening) (tangled)

6. Gabby found Miss Wellington's _____.
   (cane) (family) (sand) (money)

7. Miss Wellington was better off without _____.
   (money) (Fritz) (Gabby) (vines) (Ross)

8. Gabby said, "It's not what your _____ is, it's what you are."
   (dog) (mystery) (trouble) (family)

9. With Fritz dead, Gabby no longer had a _____.
   (sister) (policeman) (trouble) (job)

10. To get his job back again, he wanted to give Miss Wellington another _____.
    (man) (bill) (room) (dog) (cane)

Why Was It So?

Choose the right ending for each sentence below.

1. Ross thought he never should have come back to Morgan Bay because
   (a) all he found was Lucy.
   (b) the wind made his nose hurt.
   (c) all he found there was trouble.
2. Miss Wellington told Ross she had called the police because
   (a) she had.
   (b) she wanted to frighten him.
3. The police would not let Gabby keep the money from the boxes because
   (a) they wanted it.
   (b) it was no good.
   (c) it was Ross Morgan's money.
4. Vinny knew the twenty-dollar bills were not good because
   (a) the N was missing from the name Morgan.
   (b) the money came from a paper bag.
   (c) the N was missing from the name Jackson.

To Think about and Talk about

How might the story have turned out if
(a) Bill had not gone to the castle with Gabby the first night?
(b) Gabby had turned the money over to the police right away?
(c) Miss Wellington had told the police about Ross Morgan years before?

WORD LIST

Running words in *The Mystery of Morgan Castle*, the first book of the MORGAN BAY MYSTERIES, total 7,348. The number of different words used is 286. The entire vocabulary is listed below. Following each word is the number of the page on which it first appears.

Of the 286 words listed, 269 should be familiar to children reading at second-grade level. The remaining 17 (italicized in the list below) are enrichment words, necessary to the color and context of the story.

a	1	bark	9	*cane*	7	even	20
about	2	*basement*	27	can't	1	eyes	1
above	3	Bay	2	car	19		
across	7	be	3	*castle*	3	falling	10
afraid	6	beach	3	caught	13	family	6
after	3	before	6	chain	7	fast	9
again	3	behind	8	climb	12	feel	7
all	2	*bet*	20	close	1	fence	3
almost	6	better	23	come	3	find	23
alone	8	between	30	could	3	fool	54
along	3	big	3			for	2
always	1	Bill	1	dark	3	found	6
am	8	bills	17	day	8	frighten	6
an	7	blowing	7	dead	6	Fritz	1
and	1	board	2	did	1	from	8
another	13	box	28	died	19	front	12
any	1	boy	2	do	1		
are	1	branch	13	dog	2	Gabby	1
around	7	broken	6	dollar	17	garden	12
as	1	brother	1	don't	1	*gardener*	27
at	2	but	1	door	3	gate	25
away	1	by	24	down	2	get	1
						give	1
back	9	call	2	easy	2	go	7
bag	15	came	3	empty	3	gone	10
bang	7	can	2	end	3	good	20

Word	Count	Word	Count	Word	Count	Word	Count
got	17	knew	20	not	3	said	1
growl	7	know	1	nothing	12	sand	9
				now	2	saw	2
ha	54	lady	7			say	2
had	3	last	3	of	1	sea	3
hand	2	left	13	off	9	see	2
has	16	let	9	oh	1	seem	6
have	1	light	24	old	1	*shaggy*	3
he	1	like	6	on	2	she	7
hear	7	listen	1	once	2	should	16
help	40	little	3	one	1	side	7
her	7	long	6	only	3	sister	18
here	8	look	2	open	2	sitting	2
high	3	Lucy	8	or	8	*sniffed*	7
him	3			other	6	so	9
his	1	*ma'am*	8	out	8	some	6
home	15	made	6	over	3	someone	7
house	3	make	13			something	6
how	1	man	2	paper	2	sound	7
hurt	19	*married*	19	people	6	start	2
		maybe	29	picked	17	still	7
I	1	me	15	pointed	3	stood	7
if	1	men	28	police	7	stop	2
I'm	2	Miss	8	policeman	60	street	3
in	6	money	1	pull	10	Summers	1
into	7	more	7	push	15	*surf*	3
is	8	Morgan	2	put	8	*surfboard*	1
it	2	mouth	15				
it's	2	move	2	ran	3	take	9
		mystery	22	right	1	*tangle*	13
Jackson	66			river	19	tap	7
job	1	name	6	road	19	than	6
jump	9	never	1	roof	3	that	2
just	2	night	18	room	42	*that's*	1
		no	1	Ross	19	the	1
keep	10	nose	7	run	1	them	6

then	7	*toward*	13	waiting	15	who	19
there	1	town	8	walk	2	why	2
they	3	tree	3	wall	3	will	1
thing	16	trouble	9	want	1	wind	7
think	1	truck	27	was	1	window	3
this	2	twenty	17	watch	10	with	2
thought	3	two	8	way	1	without	1
three	36			we	20	would	2
through	2	under	13	well	1		
time	6	up	1	Wellington	6	years	3
tire	50	us	9	went	2	yes	2
to	1			were	3	you	1
told	1	vines	13	what	1	your	1
too	9	Vinny	18	when	8		
took	7	voice	7	where	17		